The WIZARD OF OZ

Written
and
Illustrated
by

MARK CHRISTIANSEN

Based on the classic story by L. Frank Baum

For Nonita (Annette), a blessing from God in my life.

The Wizard of Oz

linktr.ee/markscartoonart

There once was a little girl named Dorothy who lived happily on a farm in Kansas with her Uncle Henry and Aunt Em. Toto was the name of her cute little pet dog.

One day a tornado came. Uncle Henry and Aunt Em told Dorothy to join them in the cellar to be safe. But before Dorothy and Toto could get there, the tornado swooped up the house and lifted it into the sky!

Dorothy and Toto were very afraid.

The spinning house suddenly landed with a thud! Dorothy and Toto stepped outside and were greeted by three little men.

"I'm Dorothy and this is my dog, Toto," she said. "Who are you and where am I?"

One of the men said, "You are in Oz, and we are the leaders of the Munchkins. Your house landed on the Wicked Witch of the East, and now her evil power over us has been broken. We thank you!"

"I don't understand," said Dorothy. "I didn't mean to hurt anyone."

Then Glinda the Good Princess appeared. She had magic powers and was a friend to the Munchkins. Glinda showed Dorothy that the house had indeed landed on the Wicked Witch of the East.

"We are very grateful to you for breaking the Witch's evil spell, Dorothy," said Glinda. "Please tell us if we can do anything for you in return."

Dorothy said, "What I really want is to go back home to Kansas. Can you take me there?"

"I'm so sorry, Dorothy," said Glinda, "but I don't have the power to take you back to Kansas. Go see the Wizard of Oz in the Emerald City. He should be able to help you."

"How do I find the Emerald City?" asked Dorothy.

Glinda replied, "Just follow the road made of yellow bricks, and it will lead you to the Wizard of Oz. And Dorothy, I will be watching over you while you are on your journey."

So Dorothy and Toto were on their way to the Emerald City.
"I sure hope the Wizard of Oz will be able to help us get back home to Kansas, Toto," said Dorothy. "I want to see my Uncle Henry and Aunt Em again!"

As Dorothy and Toto were walking along, they heard a voice say, "Hello, how are you?" Dorothy looked up, and saw a talking scarecrow!

"Hi Scarecrow, how are you?" asked Dorothy.

"I'm not well. It's uncomforatble being tied to this pole," said the Scarecrow. "Could you please untie me and help me down?"

"Of course I will," said Dorothy.

Dorothy untied the Scarecrow and helped him get down.

"Thank you," said the Scarecrow. "What is your name and where are you going?"

"My name is Dorothy and this is my dog, Toto," she said. "We're on our way to see the Wizard of Oz because we want him to help us get back home to Kansas."

"Do you think the Wizard could give me a brain?" asked the Scarecrow. "I really want one."

Dorothy said, "Join us and you can ask the Wizard for a brain. We would love to have your company."

So Dorothy, Toto and the Scarecrow were on their way to see the Wizard of Oz!

After walking for a while, they discovered a man made of tin who was holding an axe and couldn't move because he was rusted. The Scarecrow found the Tin Woodman's oil can and began to oil his arms and legs so he could move again.

Dorothy explained to the Tin Woodman they were going to see the Wizard of Oz to ask him to help her get back to Kansas and to give the Scarecrow a brain.

"Thank you for rescuing me," said the Tin Woodman. "May I go with you to see the Wizard so I can ask him for a heart? The tinsmith who made me forgot to give me one."

He opened a little door in his chest to show that it was empty inside.

"Yes, please join us!" said Dorothy.

So the Tin Woodman joined Dorothy, the Scarecrow and Toto. They were on their way to see the Wizard!

As they walked through the forest, a lion suddenly jumped out at them and began to chase poor little Toto!

"I'm going to get you!" yelled the Lion.

Dorothy ran up and slapped the Lion on the nose.

"Don't you dare hurt my dog!" said Dorothy.

The Lion began to cry and said, "Why did you hit me? I didn't hurt your dog."

"No, but you were trying to," said Dorothy. "You should be ashamed of yourself. You're just a big coward!"

The Lion said, "You're right, I am a coward. Oh, how I would love to have some courage!"

"Come along with us," said Dorothy. "We're on our way to ask the Wizard of Oz for help. You should ask the Wizard for some courage."

"That sounds wonderful," said the Lion.

A little bit later, Dorothy and her friends arrived at the Emerald City where the Wizard of Oz lived. The Wizard's castle was sparkling green.

They asked one of the guards if they could see the Wizard.

"I'm sorry," said the guard, "but no one is allowed to see the Wizard of Oz."

"But Glinda the Good Princess sent me here," said Dorothy.

The guard said, "If Glinda sent you, then you can see the Wizard right away."

They entered the Wizard's throne room and asked him for his help.

"I'll see what I can do for you," said the Wizard. "But first, I want you to do something for me."

"What do you want us to do?" asked Dorothy.

The Wizard said, "Dorothy, I heard how you got rid of the Wicked Witch of the East. Now her sister, the Wicked Witch of the West, is using her own evil power in the Land of Oz. I want you to stop her."

"But Mr. Wizard," said Dorothy, "how are we going to do that? We don't have another house to drop on her."

"I don't know," replied the Wizard. "But you must get rid of her somehow before I can grant your requests."

Dorothy and her friends left the Emerald City to find the Wicked Witch of the West. They still didn't know how they were going to get rid of her.

"The sign says the Witch's castle is this way," said Dorothy.

"I'm sc-sc-scared," said the Lion.

"We're all scared," said the Tin Woodman.

The Wicked Witch of the West was looking out her castle window and saw Dorothy and her friends.

"That's the little girl whose house landed on my sister!" said the Witch. "Well, I'm not going to let her destroy me too!"

The Witch called for the leader of the Winged Monkeys.
"I want you and the other Winged Monkeys to bring that girl and her friends to me right now!" said the Witch.

All the Winged Monkeys went out and captured Dorothy, Toto, the Scarecrow, the Tin Woodman and the Lion.

"Somebody please help us!" screamed Dorothy.

The Winged Monkeys brought them to the castle.

"Put the Scarecrow, Tin Woodman and Lion in the dungeon," the Witch told the Monkeys.

"Please let us go!" Dorothy said.

"You're not going anywhere," said the Witch. "From now on, you will be my prisoner and do chores around the castle. Start washing the floor!"

Toto growled at the Witch.

"Growl at me, will you?" said the Witch to Toto. "Maybe I'll turn you into a frog!"

Then the Witch cackled with laughter.

That angered Dorothy.

"Put Toto down this instant!" she yelled.

And then Dorothy picked up the bucket of water and threw it at the Wicked Witch.

"Why did you do that to me?" screamed the Witch. "Now I'm going to melt away!"

Dorothy said, "I'm sorry! I didn't know that would happen!"

After the Witch melted away, all that was left were her hat and shoes.

"Look at that, Toto!" exclaimed Dorothy. "I can't believe it!"

The Wicked Witch of the West was gone!

The leader of the Winged Monkeys said to Dorothy, "Thank you for breaking the evil spell the Wicked Witch of the West had over us! Here are the Witch's magic shoes. We want you to have them. She used the shoes for evil, but you can use them for good."

Dorothy unlocked the jail cell and freed the Scarecrow, the Tin Woodman and the Lion.

"Let's go!" said Dorothy. "The Winged Monkeys are going to take us back to the Emerald City!"

So the Winged Monkeys brought Dorothy and the others back to the Wizard's castle.

"I and all the people of Oz thank you for getting rid of the Wicked Witch of the West!" said the Wizard. "Now the time has come for me to grant your requests."

The Wizard gave the Scarecrow a magic potion to drink that made him smart.

The Tin Woodman got a mechanical heart from the Wizard.

And the Lion got his courage from a magic medal that the Wizard gave him.

Then the Wizard said to Dorothy, "I'm so sorry my dear, but I just don't know how to send you back home to Kansas. You and Toto are welcome to stay here in Oz. The Scarecrow, Tin Woodman, Lion and I will take good care of you."

Dorothy began to cry. "Thank you, Mr. Wizard," she said, "but I miss my Uncle Henry and Aunt Em. I want to be with them!"

Suddenly, Glinda the Good Princess appeared.
She said, "Don't cry, Dorothy. You have the power to go back to Kansas now. Just put on the magic shoes that used to belong to the Wicked Witch of the West and wish that you were back home."
Dorothy said, "That's wonderful, Glinda. Thank you!"

Dorothy put on the magic shoes
"We're going to miss you," said the Scarecrow.
"And I'm going to miss you all," said Dorothy.
After saying goodbye to the Scarecrow, Tin Woodman
and Lion, Dorothy held Toto closely and said, "I want
to go back home to Kansas."

In an instant, Dorothy and Toto were being carried in the sky by a whirlwind! They were on their way back to Kansas!

When they arrived at the Kansas farm, Dorothy ran up to her Aunt Em and hugged her. Uncle Henry came running toward them.

Aunt Em said, "Oh, Dorothy, we were so worried about you! We're so thankful you're home safe!"

And Dorothy was very happy to be back home with her Uncle Henry and Aunt Em!

Made in the USA
Monee, IL
25 September 2023

43316764R00024